THE HUNTSMAN

A dark Snow White short story

Des Fonoimoana

CONTENTS

1

R*UN… RUN!*

The sensation of fire courses through every vein in my body, burning my lungs with each breath that I struggle to take. My legs tremble beneath me and I can feel perspiration dotting my forehead as exhaustion works against me. Everything around me is hazy as the lack of food and water over the past few days takes its toll. I want to fall and lie down and sleep for many nights on the leaf-covered floor of the forest.

But I know that I can't. I must survive.

I've tried to only focus on the distance between myself and the horror that I'm running from. Occasionally, I squint to avoid the power of the sun as I study its place in the sky, seeing that almost an hour has passed by. My feet grow numb in my boots and I push myself to be faster. An extra inch of distance could be the difference between life and death.

"You have one hour before I release my hounds and ride," were all the guidelines

that I received. I didn't need much more information because I knew what was coming. I knew that death followed me like an old friend. What happens in the woods surrounding our kingdom is common knowledge.

And I might be the most naïve person for agreeing to it.

I volunteered myself in a roundabout way, making myself into a problem and getting dragged away by the queen's guards. No amount of their beating, torture, or threats made me regret their choice because I was able to protect my siblings from their wrath. At least this time.

"Thalia you cannot think this way! You must survive!" I growl to myself. "You must *live*."

This sprint that I've been doing for nearly an hour seems short when I consider the four-legged hounds that will follow me soon. There are seven of them—all vicious, nearly-starved males. They haven't been fed much over the past week and they know they're about to eat well. Each dog is more determined than the last, making them a dangerous enemy. If I have to say one good thing about those rotten mutts, it's that they are hardworking and have never, ever lost a hunt.

The hounds will hunt me to the ends of the earth and wherever they corner me will be the place that I take my last breath. Maybe I'll die in their strong jaws or maybe I'll be taken at the end of a blade, but I am fearful for a fate worse than death.

I fear he is planning something that lasts for days, until death is the only escape that I'm hungry for. I am his greatest hunt. And I know he is planning the greatest end for my life.

It will depend on how he feels… how The Huntsman feels.

And the word is that he is not feeling very merciful after his favorite whore left town with his brother. Shame, I might have lived a few extra days if he had been tracking them instead.

I know what I have to live for and I must hold onto that. I have to fight and protect my siblings, no matter the cost, even if the cost is my life.

2

So much for hospitality: a dark, damp, and poor smelling cell is my home, until they decide that it's not anymore. The smell of piss and rotting human faeces makes me want to vomit. I spend my time covering my face with my shirt, unable to escape those scents and the worst scent of all—blood.

The torture chamber sits next to my cell, a common room for the guests with monthly rates. Those who will be stuck in here include petty criminals and prisoners of war who face the dangerous wrath of the queen. Though their crimes may differ, their screams of pain all sound the same.

My crime is being a woman. The Huntsman said: "a beautiful one, much to the envy of the queen." I wonder if that's the truth or a lie. I'm starving, shaking, and know that my face has sunken in. I'm not beautiful, if I ever had been. But thinking of the women in the past, taken from their homes in the kingdom, they've all been beautiful.

Dark hair, pale skin, bright eyes… becoming in every way.

And they were hunted like animals.

I rest my head against the cell and cover my ears, hearing a man howl in pain. It sends shivers down my spine and I feel alert and nauseous. I cannot fathom what is happening next to me, even when I hear the roar of a fire or the turn of a crank. I refuse to imagine what they are suffering through as I remain unharmed. It's a selfish thought. My karma, I suppose, will be the hunt.

A fist slams against the cell door and I jump, staring into the ravenous eyes of The Huntsman. He looks satisfied with my lack of freedom. He studies me, feeling fulfilled when he notices my fear.

"You are the first," he purrs.

I ignore him, turning away and staring at the dark wall across from me. It's more appealing than this bastard could ever be. I am, nevertheless, curious what that means. *The first*. Hmph.

"You are the first to ever sacrifice yourself. I know that is what you did." His voice is deep, sinister. Whatever he thinks I am doing, he's feeding off it. "You were saving your sisters."

I steal a glimpse of him and he smirks.

"But for how long?"

I'm already dead so I grab my plate and the disgusting pile of muck on it and throw it against the cell. He manages to dodge the food and smiles. I've just made this more enticing for him. My fire and drive will make his hunt a rewarding one.

"I have hunted hundreds of beautiful women. None have been as thrilling as I know you will be. I cannot wait to strangle the life from you."

He rests against the cell once more, leaning nonchalantly and picking at a hangnail. He plans to irritate me more.

He wants this to be more of a challenge for him. I refuse to reward him.

I pull myself into a ball to appear scared until he grows bored and pushes himself away from the cell bars.

"Once you're gone, there will be no one to save them." He gives me a sly smile and leaves me with nothing but the words that echo in my head. A warning, a threat, a promise.

All I know is that I cannot be another trophy for this man.

3

I DID NOT EXPECT to be blinded by the sun when they dragged me from my cage and into the daylight. I had fallen to my knees and hid my face, blocking it from the brightness. It hurts, more than the ache in my stomach or the throbbing in my head.

I have to overcome the pain. If I don't overcome the pain, I will not survive.

And if I do not survive, my sisters will face the same fate that I face today. Only I imagine, to spite me, The Huntsman will make their deaths worse.

At least I'm not stuck in a cell any longer. I am free, even though I'll be hunted to the ends of the earth.

I gaze upwards, trying to ignore the sticker bush that snatches at my skin and pulls the flesh from my legs. The sun is ahead of me now, beating down on my face to remind me what troubles will track me down. Even as long as I have sprinted, I know there's not much distance between me and the city behind. The hounds will be released soon enough.

I am frantic when I realize that I may only have minutes left. How will I hide my scent from those dogs? How can I cover all the tracks that lay behind me? My heart pounds in my chest harder and harder until I feel lightheaded. I stumble and I fall, my hands striking the half-dried mud. I clench it in despair, trying to fight back tears. I have to stay clear-headed, enough to hide myself.

It hits me as the mud sinks underneath my fingernails. I scoop some up with a weird sense of relief and eagerness, and begin to slather the mud onto my skin, my arms, my hair, and my clothes. As fast as I can, I hide my scent under the earthy layer, making sure to cover my sweat glands.

A howl echoes through the forest and my head jerks in the direction of the noise. I grunt and push myself up, trying to convince my legs that they are not wobbly, or tired, or exhausted. The goal is to get my adrenaline and my desire to survive to overpower my hurting muscles. The seven hounds will be upon me soon enough.

I know that he's far away, but I swear I can hear the laughter of The

Huntsman, echoing through the trees as he prepares for his hunt.

4

I KNOW ALMOST TWO dozen women who have been killed under the orders of the queen. At least, those are only the ones that I could name. Their faces were engraved into my mind. We wept for them, prayed for them, and mourned for the wickedness that they endured. Many other women died this way, but I do not remember all of their names or faces. I only remember the screams of their loved ones that were drowned out by the howls of the hounds.

Their names pass through my mind. *Ersa…. Chloris… Kathika… Isleen…* I say a promise to each of them, their faces seemingly fading from my memory.

"I will avenge you… I will live," I whisper into the air. They died for pure wickedness and nothing more. Our town, in the shadow of the castle, has suffered greatly from the loss of these women. No more. Not another mother or father, sibling, or friend, will lose a woman to The Huntsman and the queen. I cannot allow it. If I can turn the tables, I can avenge them. All I need is a weapon.

Barks reverberate behind me, skipping across the trees. The hounds seem hungry. They long for a bite of flesh, their liberation granted at the gates where they can finally hunt. I hear a chanting above the noises of the hounds and a shiver runs down my spine.

The Huntsman.

The noises stop—I know they've lost my trail in the mud. At least, for the time being. These damn hounds are smarter than the average dog and they're hungry for the blood of a human. Trained, beaten, and transformed by The Huntsman himself, they are powerful and bloodthirsty killers, only controlled by The Huntsman and the queen. The chances of escaping the hounds are slim to none. I will be hound kibble soon enough.

I scold myself for thinking that way, for thinking that I have no power or choice in my future. For thinking the worst. That is not me. I am a fighter; for the length of time that I was trapped in a cell, even then I made myself look for the light at the end of the tunnel.

Though the hope that stuck with me then is threatening to abandon me now.

I push on through my doubt and time goes by slowly, but I feel confident about the lead that I have. I might escape, I might survive. I might see tomorrow.

As the thoughts of freedom grace me, I feel something grab me from behind and whirl me around.

I muffle a scream by biting my lip as I spin with an outstretched hand, losing a breath when I realize who has grabbed me.

"Florian?" My voice cracks, my dry lips forming the syllables. My heart flutters

when his hands grasp mine, his face pale white. "What are you doing in the woods?"

He pulls his brows together as if I should know. "Rescuing you," he says, glancing over his shoulder. "We have to get out of here."

I don't know what to say. I nod, allowing him to pull me behind him, moving swiftly through the trees. My head races with thoughts. How did he find me? What are we going to do? What if The Huntsman takes his life as punishment for helping me?

I squeeze tighter as he helps me over a fallen log and through the dirt and leaves along the forest floor. I want to ask him what his plan is—why his brow looks so intent as he pulls me. There is something heavy on his mind and I think maybe it's survival. We're in this together.

Florian does his best to keep me moving, to keep me on my feet as I struggle to meet his pace. If we slow down or I stumble, the hounds might be upon us. I can hear their whines in the distance, their noses seeking my scent. They are coming up empty and I'm not sure how long that will last. Florian's scent might catch.

"What are you planning?" I plead. "I need to know."

He shakes his head, a road appearing in front of us. I see a strong stallion standing in front of me, waggling its head in the air. "We are going back to the castle."

"*What?*"

He doesn't say anything as he yanks me up onto the back of his horse and makes certain that I'm settled in, my muddy arms wrapping around him. I realize now how I smell, how disgusting I feel from my time in a cell and running for my life through the forest. Florian doesn't seem to notice, or doesn't seem to care.

"We are going to kill the queen and The Huntsman."

"Why are we killing your mother?" I demand. "Why can we not just run away?"

He growls. "Because if she is alive, these massacres will *never* stop," he spits. "Normally she traps me in my room but I managed to escape. To save you."

I freeze in disbelief. He wants to kill his mother… the queen? Has this been something that he's wanted for a long time? Will he be punished for this scheme? It doesn't matter. My only option is to help him. This might be my way to avenge those that we have lost, and the fire burning inside of him only makes me want to help more.

"What is your plan? Tell me everything, Florian," I say. I wipe the mud off of my face, the dry patches pulling the skin of my cheeks tight. My arms shake at my sides, the dried earth dropping off as we ride.

"They will be scouring the forests for you until nightfall. It will give us time to gather ourselves and when they return to the castle, that's when we strike. They'll never anticipate you being in the castle with her. And we can kill The Huntsman when he enters." His voice is dark and angry—a terrorizing thing. He has never held this rage inside of him. "I have a friend not far from the castle. We'll go there."

I don't mean to, but I feel the tears falling from my eyes and I begin to sob against his back. The grief, fear, and the relief of being saved washes over me. I haven't had a moment to really *feel* emotions and my entire body shakes as they course through me.

Florian looks back over his shoulder, sighing when he sees the redness of my eyes and the streaks of mud on my cheeks. I hope he doesn't look at me with pity, but relief, too. He never has before and he best not start now.

We ride in silence for a long while, away from the heart of the forest and the pained howls of the hounds that have lost my scent, their hunger worsening. The horse is faster than the hounds, leaving my smell far behind in the woods and putting precious space between us and the hounds.

This is not new; Florian saving me. We would play throughout the village together as children and my mighty temper outweighed my tiny body. I would always cause fights with bigger kids for pulling at my braids and snickering about my shoes with holes in them, or simply because they were cocky imbeciles. Florian always came to my rescue, sending them off with his guards and offering to buy me new shoes. I declined, but he never stopped offering. He never stopped saving me: from boys that didn't take no for an answer, to keeping me safe from a bear… it's no surprise that he's saved me now and my gratitude becomes deeper and deeper with every passing second.

After a long while, we reach a cottage at the foot of the mountain range. A small trail of smoke curls up into the sky, disappearing into the thick canopy above. There is a small garden to the side of the house and a coup for chickens. A quaint place, making me wonder why we are here even more.

Florian pushes himself up and off the horse, offering me a hand when he's firmly on the ground. "Come on, we'll be safe here."

I swallow nervously but I take his hand, struggling to push my tired body off the horse by myself. He holds me close, offering to support me if I need it. I try to be strong and reliant only on myself as we approach the cottage and Florian knocks on the wood door.

It takes a few minutes of standing there in apprehension before the door opens slightly, a long, crooked nose poking out to analyze us. A grey-haired woman opens the door enough to reveal her smoky eyes, fading into blindness. She can see enough to know that Florian stands in front of her.

"Please, come inside, Grandson. And bring your friend. Hurry." She steps back, opening the door just enough for us to slip in and then she slams it shut and locks it securely.

Florian ushers me in and has me sit, grabbing a mug and filling it with water from a pitcher that sits in the center of the table, next to a bowl of shiny, red apples. I am eager to drink, the water running down my cheeks as I gulp down the water until my stomach aches. I don't know how I'm alive, but by the gods I'm grateful. The look in my dear friend's eyes tells me that I look as horrid as I feel right now. Exhausted, shaky, anxious… but grateful.

My mug is refilled without asking for it. I grab it and drink and drink until the whole pitcher is empty.

"How will you do it, Grandson?"

I realize, when I gaze upon her face fully, for the first time, that this woman is the old queen. The one who was envious and vulgar and taken off the throne. Now she looks softer, more gentle as she pats her grandson's face gingerly. Such a terrifying woman has become a loving grandmother. Still I cannot fight the thought that she looks beaten down. I wonder what led her to be like this.

"We will sneak in and kill her. And then The Huntsman. I am going to dress her like a maid and get her inside." He exhales angrily, gesturing to me. "I can't believe that it's come to this. I didn't know it had gotten so bad, but my mother and The Huntsman do as they please. Slaughtering the women in our kingdom."

I see the grandmother pat her grandson on the arm again. "It is not your fault, Florian. You are doing the right thing."

She reaches under the table, pulling out a long, thin item in a bag and handing it to him. "This poison will insure their deaths, Florian."

A poisoned blade.

He swallows hard and nods. He knows the weight that this burden will carry and though it's difficult, he knows he must do it. It is the right thing to do to save the lives of many others.

The darkness in his eyes pulls at me and I blurt, "I'll do it. I will kill them."

My dear friend freezes in place, his mouth falling open when my words register. "You would kill them?" he asks in disbelief. "You don't have to take on that burden. It's my responsibility to stop them."

"I want to do it," I say. "I want to be the last person they see before they die. After what I went through and what all those women went through… I think it would be the sweetest revenge if I killed them. Please let me."

Florian swallows hard and hands me the blade. "Okay. You'll be the one to take their lives."

5

REST HAS DONE ME well, no matter how little I have gotten in the cabin. Florian took the time to help braid my hair as best he could and hide me in a cloak with an eye patch, allowing me to go under the guise of a servant. The grandmother allowed me the chance to clean up before we left and I removed the smells of the castle and the forest, praying for the strength to do what needs to be done during this time.

"I wish I had seen the evil of my own ways long before I did. It is a shame, though, that my daughter never will," she had whispered to me. It was her way of telling me that she will forgive me for what I had to do. I clenched the blade tightly to my chest and gave her a strong nod. It *will* be done.

Florian stays by my side as we enter the castle yard, guarding my face from any onlookers who bow to him. We make our way inside, my heart pounding in my throat as I realize what's coming. I try to stay calm for him and hide how anxious I am. I'd gotten good at this game—appearing composed when I'm frantic on the inside.

We make our way to his apartments, the guards giving him suggestive smiles. It wasn't uncommon for the royals to take servants to bed. I wonder, as he allows me inside his rooms, if Florian does such things.

"Stay quiet," he orders, locking his door and walking to his window. He peers out, seeing the courtyard below. His mother and The Huntsman cross it hurriedly; angry and exchanging hushed words. "They will be meeting in her chambers."

"Are you saying they are—"

"—Yes. They've been lovers for many years," he mutters with disgust. "I wonder if The Huntsman is my real father sometimes. Mother will never give me a straight answer."

I furrow my brow. "Florian it does not change who you are if he's your father. You are an incredibly kind person and the kingdom will be lucky to have you as their king one day."

He stays quiet and moves away from the window, going to his cabinets and gathering supplies. He grabs an array of daggers and other blades in case he needs them. He hands a few of them to me and I slide them up my sleeves, hoping that they look discreet. We have to prepare for what is to come. And anything could take us by surprise.

6

"Y OU READY?" FLORIAN WHISPERS to me. He pushes the door open a crack, peering inside.

I can hear the faint whispers of the queen and her huntsman. They seem angry even in the quietness of their voices. Their whispers are harsh and sharp. The Huntsman is getting blamed for allowing me to escape. His failed hunt. Me. The only hunt that he has ever lost.

That realization is bittersweet. On one hand, I am grateful to be alive and to have outlived his torture. On the other hand, I ache for the women who have lost their lives before me, for their families who have had to learn how to live without them… Without ever being able to seek the justice that they desire. I'm doing this for them more than myself.

And for the women who haven't died by The Huntsman's hand, but are still afflicted by him… I will do this for them too. It is not uncommon for families to mutilate their daughters to make them unattractive and protect them from the fate of being *the fairest of them all*. It is sickening that they believe mutilation is the only way to protect them. I cannot imagine being stuck in that hell.

"I am," I say.

I catch his gaze momentarily, giving him a nod before I put my hand in front of him, push the door open and slam it behind me, leaving him on the other side. I lock it quickly, hearing his protests as I keep him safe on the other side. He knows, though, that if he makes a scene it will risk my life.

It is better that he's locked out anyway. I don't want him to have to take his own mother's life. And I certainly don't want him to freeze when he has the chance to take it.

My breath catches in my throat as I listen to the queen and The Huntsman challenge one another. They do not notice me as they snarl back and forth; they believe me to be a servant and that allows me enough time to get closer to them, inconspicuously.

"I cannot believe you lost the hunt," the queen growls at him. "Pathetic excuse for a man! Are you capable of doing *anything* right?"

For a split second my heart aches for him facing this verbiage, until I recall all the horrid things that he's done. Mutilated, tortured, and abused women for years and years. I cannot pity such a monster. There is no chance that I will forgive him. I will not feel for him. He deserves any mistreatment that she gives him.

Rage overcomes me when the memories return.

I step closer to them, my hand gripping the hilt of the poisoned blade. I am ready to end this. Justice for those women we lost is my goal today; that and a better future for the little girls like my sister who could one day be in my shoes. I don't care what my future becomes, so long as The hunt does not become theirs.

With a quick step, my hand goes up and comes down in a single swift motion, the blade meeting the soft, human flesh as it pulls towards the ground. There's a horrible tearing sound and I feel lightheaded, not understanding how human skin can make that noise. I nearly gag, but then the sounds stop. Silence and confusion envelop me and I realize that the knife is stuck in The Huntsman's shoulder.

I did that. I stabbed him with the intent to kill. For a moment, I'm stunned that I had the nerve to do it.

It is only enough to shock him.

I release the dagger—stupidly—and step away, putting a table between myself and The Huntsman and queen before they comprehend what I've done. Neither of them say anything at first as they process the scene, until The Huntsman's face twists to a devious smirk. I've poked the bear with a dagger and his newfound goal is to make me wish that I had died in that forest. I am in serious danger if he captures me.

"So, this was your scheme? You volunteered so you could attempt to kill me?"

"It simply fell into place," I murmur, "I can't say I'm not grateful for the opportunity."

He snarls at my derisiveness and flings himself over the table with terrifying speed towards me. I move quicker than he can react and I press myself against the wall that he slams himself into. He manages to hit me with a kick, causing me to howl in pain from the blow to my hip. I ignore it just long enough to move further away from him.

"What is that disgusting girl doing in here?!" The queen is bellowing, hiding behind her huntsman.

"You're not as scary without your hounds," I say to The Huntsman, disregarding her. "But you will die like a dog for all the hurt and suffering you've caused."

"You can *try*," he snarls at me. "After I lock you back up, I'm going to let every guard have their way with you until you're too weak to have any fight left in you. That's when the hounds will devour your family. In front of your eyes. You will watch every bite and gash and you will listen to every scream until it is burned into your mind. You've sealed the deal, wench. You will stay alive and listen to the sounds of my prey in pain for the rest of your days."

He comes for me again and I dart out of the way in a panic. This time he crashes, his body smashing into a full length mirror on the wall, surrounded by beautiful flowers and golden decor. It is clearly important, having been adorned like a shrine. When it falls across the floor, it shatters into thousands of pieces, shards sliding every which way.

His eyes drop to the shards and he gasps, his face drained of color at the sight. The queen shrieks as though she's in horrifying pain and lunges after him. With a quick movement she tears the dagger from his shoulder and pins him against the wall in a second. The blade is placed against his throat.

"You *bastard*! You broke it! How dare you! You broke my precious mirror!"

"It was an accident, Snow, you must believe me, my love," he pleads. "Please."

The blade is pressing hard enough against his skin that it breaks open and dots of blood drip down his throat and collarbone. Something inside her has snapped and her control has vanished.

Either way, the poison has entered his system and if she doesn't kill him first, the blade will.

She is screaming at him and cursing him over and over… then the blade digs into his gut. A pained gurgle leaves his throat.

I gasp, stunned that she is willing to take his life over a *mirror*. He is wordless, but his eyes are wide with shock as blood pools from his mouth and his stomach. She is ending his life faster than the poison ever could.

His calloused hand snatches the air and touches nothing. He falls to the floor with a thud, going lifeless, and she hovers above him, every breath shaking her body with anger.

I know now that I'm next. I have no weapon, no chance at fighting off the queen in my weakened state. I need to defend myself… but perhaps I should attack her before she has the chance to recover from what happened to her mirror?

The mirror. The shards are scattered across the floor. I snatch one up before I doubt myself and it tears open the skin of my palm. But it doesn't matter now. My adrenaline is too high for me to care. I sprint towards her and plunge the shard directly into her temple.

My hand radiates with pain as blood streams down it. I step back, watching her face briefly contort in pain before expression leaves her face entirely. The queen is frozen in front of me for a long moment. I swear I can see her life flash in front of her eyes as her soul vacates its monstrous vessel. Shortly after I see her lip curl with hate, she collapses on top of her lover's body, little twitches coming from her limbs before it just *stops*.

My eyes go to my hand and I know that I need to wrap it up soon. I can't risk losing blood in my current state. I wrap my hand tightly in a nearby blanket and open the door to let Florian in.

He steps in, cautious, and loses his breath when he sees the bodies sprawled across the floor in a river of blood. He reaches out and places a hand on the small of my back. I know that he's trying to understand what happened in this blood filled room but at least he's released from the strangling emotions and guilt that he had.

"You did it," he whispers. "How did you manage it?"

"She killed him in a fit of rage," I say. "And when she was distracted, I used the shards of the mirror to stab her."

"That mirror was the toy she used to pick her next victim," he snarls, disgusted. "I can't believe she killed him."

I nod in agreement. None of that matters now. Florian can take his rightful place as King and make the kingdom brighter and safer than had been in centuries. No one will ever lose a child, or friend, or sibling to the queen, The Huntsman, or the hounds again.

This is it. No more torture, or pain, or devastation.

He takes my unscathed hand and gives me a reassuring nod as tears stream down my face. I am relieved and distraught, shaken up with confusion. Everything seems to come crashing down inside of me, despite the relief and gratitude that I feel for my dear friend who saved me from my death sentence.

I can see the pain in his eyes from having to wish death upon his own mother, but he seems at peace now. He can make up for her crimes and mend the things that she had broken, including the trust between the kingdom's ruler and the people. If anyone can fix it, it will be the just and kind Florian.

And I can return to my family. I can give justice to the families of those who lost their lives. Together we can make certain it never happens again, and that women will no longer live in fear of certain death.

I take a deep, filling breath for the first time in weeks. I smile.

The hunt has finally ended.

Des Fonoimoana, or Des The Writer, has been writing since she could lift a pencil (though her stories were not always legible). During the day, she works with teens that have emotional and behavioral disorders and serves the community. At night, she spends time writing, drawing, gaming, and playing guitar. And of course, spending time with her husband, Josh, corgi, Ginger, and kitty. Finnegan.

The Monsters Within and *The Monsters Emerge* are part of *The Monsters* series and are available everywhere.

To find out more information and stay up to date with news and novels, check out her social media accounts @DesTheWriter or visit DesTheWriter.com